Henry and Mudge

The First Book of Their Adventures

Story by Cynthia Rylant
Pictures by Suçie Stevenson

BRADBURY PRESS • NEW YORK

For Nate and his dog—CR

For Grandma Biffy—SS

THE HENRY AND MUDGE BOOKS

Text copyright © 1987 by Cynthia Rylant
Illustrations copyright © 1987 by Suçie Stevenson

Bradbury Press
An Affiliate of Macmillan, Inc.
866 Third Avenue, New York, N.Y. 10022
Collier Macmillan Canada, Inc.

Manufactured in the United States of America
10   9   8   7
The text of this book is set in 18 pt. Goudy Old Style.
The illustrations are watercolor and reproduced in full color.

Library of Congress Cataloging-in-Publication Data
Rylant, Cynthia. Henry and Mudge.
Summary: Henry, feeling lonely on a street without
any other children, finds companionship and love in a big dog
named Mudge.
[1. Dogs—Fiction] I. Stevenson, Suçie ill. II. Title.
PZ7.R982He 1987 [E] 86–13615
ISBN 0-02-778001-5

Contents

Henry

Henry had no brothers
and no sisters.
"I want a brother,"
he told his parents.
"Sorry," they said.
Henry had no friends
on his street.

"I want to live
on a different street,"
he told his parents.
"Sorry," they said.
Henry had no pets
at home.
"I want to have a dog,"
he told his parents.
"Sorry," they *almost* said.

But first they looked
at their house
with no brothers and sisters.
Then they looked
at their street
with no children.
Then they looked
at Henry's face.

Then they looked at each other.

"Okay," they said.

"I want to hug you!"

Henry told his parents.

And he did.

Henry searched for a dog.

"Not just any dog," said Henry.

"Not a short one," he said.

"Not a curly one," he said.

"And no pointed ears."

Then he found Mudge.
Mudge had floppy ears,
not pointed.
And Mudge had straight fur,
not curly.
But Mudge was short.
"Because he's a puppy,"
Henry said.
"He'll grow."

And did he ever!

He grew out of his puppy cage.

He grew out of his dog cage.

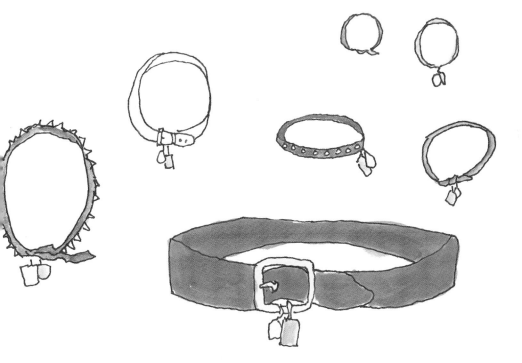

He grew out of seven collars

in a row.

And when he finally

stopped growing . . .

he weighed one hundred eighty pounds,

he stood three feet tall,

and he drooled.

"I'm glad you're not short,"

Henry said.

And Mudge licked him,
then sat on him.

Henry

Henry used to walk

to school alone.

When he walked

he used to worry about

tornadoes,

ghosts,

biting dogs,

and bullies.

He walked as fast
as he could.
He looked straight ahead.
He never looked back.
But now he walked to school
with Mudge.

And now when he walked,
he thought about
vanilla ice cream,
rain,
rocks,
and good dreams.
He walked to school
but not too fast.
He walked to school
and sometimes backward.

He walked to school
and patted Mudge's big head,
happy.

Mudge

Mudge loved Henry's room.

He loved the dirty socks.

He loved the stuffed bear.

He loved the fish tank.

But mostly he loved
Henry's bed.

Because in Henry's bed
was Henry.
Mudge loved to climb in
with Henry.
Then he loved
to smell him.

He smelled his lemon hair.

He smelled his milky mouth.

He smelled his soapy ears.

He smelled his chocolate fingers.

Then he put his head
by Henry's head.
He looked at the fish tank.
He looked at the bear.
He looked at Henry.
He licked him.
And he fell asleep.

Mudge

One day Mudge took a walk

without Henry.

The sun was shining,

the birds were flying,

the grass smelled sweet.

Mudge couldn't wait for Henry.

So he left.

He went down one road,

sniffing the bushes,

then down another road,

kicking up dust.

He went through a field,

across a stream,

into some pine trees.

And when he came out
on the other side,
he was lost.

He couldn't smell Henry.
He couldn't smell
his front porch.
He couldn't smell
the street he lived on.
Mudge looked all around
and didn't see anything
or anyone
he knew.

He whined a little,
alone without Henry.
Then he lay down,
alone without Henry.
He missed Henry's bed.

Henry

Henry thought Mudge
would be with him always.
He thought Mudge
made everything safe.
He thought Mudge
would never go away.

And when Mudge did go away,
when Henry called and called
but Mudge didn't come,
Henry's heart hurt
and he cried for an hour.
But when he finished crying,
Henry said, "Mudge loves me.
He wouldn't leave.
He must be lost."

So Henry walked and walked,
and he called and called,
and he looked and looked
for his dog Mudge.
He walked down one road,
then down another road.
The sun shone as Henry ran
through a field,
calling and calling.

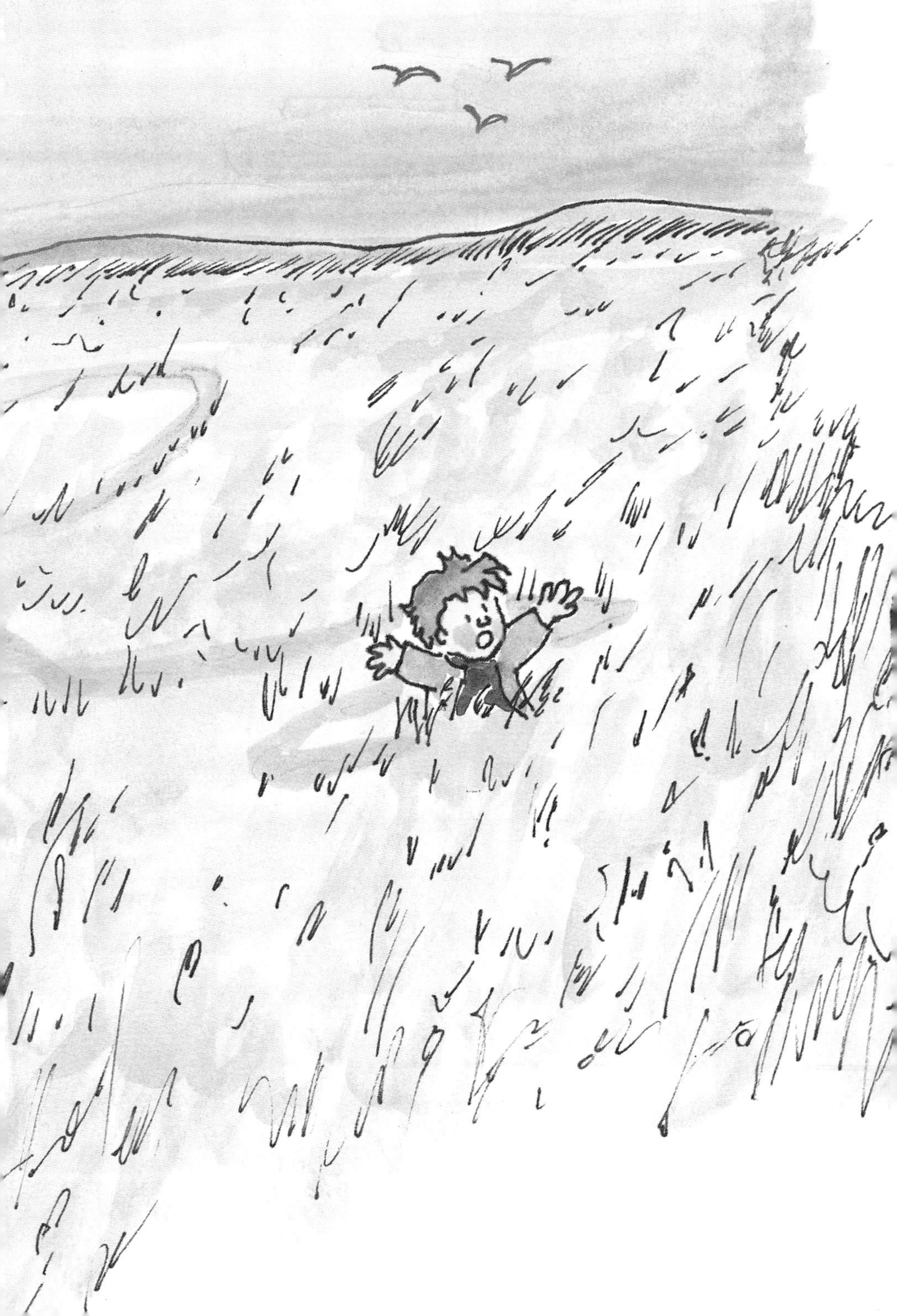

The birds flew past
as he stood beside a stream,
calling and calling.

And the tears fell again
as he looked at the
empty pine trees
for his lost dog.
"*Mudge!*" he called, one last time.

And Mudge woke up
from his lonely sleep,
then
came
running.

Henry and Mudge

Every day when Henry woke up,

he saw Mudge's big head.

And every day

when Mudge woke up,

he saw Henry's small face.

They ate breakfast
at the same time;

they ate supper
at the same time.

And when Henry was at school,
Mudge just lay around
and waited.
Mudge never went for a walk
without Henry again.
And Henry never worried
that Mudge would leave.

Because sometimes, in their dreams,
they saw long silent roads,
big wide fields,
deep streams,
and pine trees.

In those dreams,
Mudge was alone
and Henry was alone.
So when Mudge woke up
and knew Henry was with him,
he remembered the dream
and stayed closer.

And when Henry woke up
and knew Mudge was with him,
he remembered the dream
and the looking
and the calling
and the fear
and he knew
he would never lose Mudge
again.